STAR WARS™

FINN AND POE TEAM UP!

WRITTEN BY NATE MILLICI

ART BY ANDREA PARISI & GRZEGORZ KRYSINSKI

ABDO
Spotlight

Disney
LUCASFILM
P R E S S
Los Angeles • New York

ABDOPUBLISHING.COM

Reinforced library bound edition published in 2018 by Spotlight, a division of ABDO, PO Box 398166, Minneapolis, Minnesota 55439. Spotlight produces high-quality reinforced library bound editions for schools and libraries. Published by Disney • Lucasfilm Press, an imprint of Disney Book Group.

Printed in the United States of America, North Mankato, Minnesota.
042017
092017

THIS BOOK CONTAINS
RECYCLED MATERIALS

PUBLISHER'S CATALOGING-IN-PUBLICATION DATA

Names: Millici, Nate, author. | Parisi, Andrea ; Krysinski, Grzegorz, illustrator.
Title: Star wars: Finn and Poe team up! / writer: Nate Millici ; art: Andrea Parisi, Grzegorz Krysinski.
Other titles: Finn and Poe team up!
Description: Reinforced library bound edition. | Minneapolis, Minnesota : Spotlight, 2018. | Series: World of reading level 1
Summary: Finn and Poe team up to escape from the evil First Order.
Identifiers: LCCN 2017936172 | ISBN 9781532140549 (lib. bdg.)
Subjects: LCSH: Star Wars fiction--Comic book, strips, etc.--Juvenile fiction. | Space warfare--Juvenile fiction. | Adventure and adventurers--Juvenile fiction. Graphic novels--Juvenile fiction.
Classification: DDC [Fic]--dc23
LC record available at https://lccn.loc.gov/2017936172

Spotlight
A Division of ABDO
abdopublishing.com

Poe was a pilot.
He fought against
the evil First Order.

One day, Leia gave Poe
a special mission.

Poe and his droid, BB-8, needed to find a man named Lor San Tekka.

The First Order wanted
to find Lor San Tekka, too.
But one stormtrooper did not
want to go on the mission.
His name was FN-2187.

Lor San Tekka lived on
a planet called Jakku.
Poe and BB-8 flew to Jakku.
The First Order ships
also flew to Jakku.

Poe found Lor San Tekka first.
Lor San Tekka gave Poe a map.
The map would help Leia
find her brother, Luke.

Luke was a great Jedi Knight. Leia thought that Luke could help stop the First Order.

The First Order troopers
landed on Jakku.

The First Order troopers
looked for Lor San Tekka.

Poe told Lor San Tekka to hide.
Poe gave the map to BB-8.
Poe did not want the
First Order to find the map.

FN-2187 did not want to
hurt the people on Jakku.
FN-2187 did not want to hurt anyone.

The troopers captured Poe.
They took Poe to Kylo Ren.

Kylo Ren wanted the map.
Kylo Ren was angry when
Poe did not have the map.

The First Order troopers took
Poe back to their ship.
Poe was locked in a prison cell.

Captain Phasma was mad at FN-2187.

Kylo Ren made Poe tell him
where the map was hidden.
Poe told Kylo Ren that BB-8
had the map.

FN-2187 did not want
to be a part of the First Order.
But FN-2187 needed help.

FN-2187 freed Poe.
They would escape
the First Order as a team!

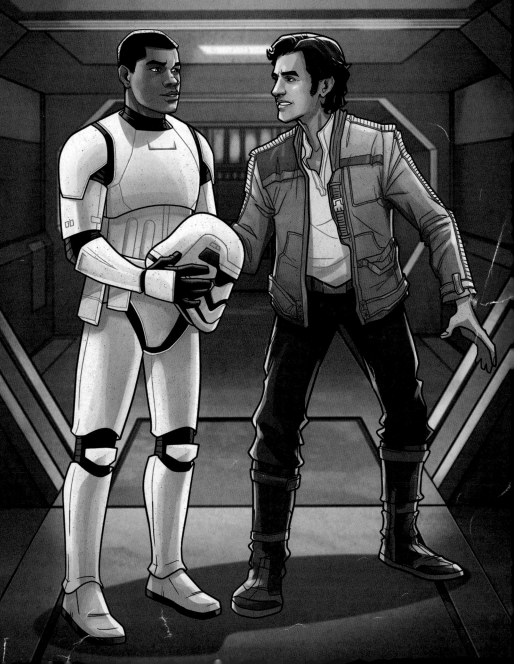

FN-2187 and Poe stole a TIE fighter.
But the troopers put up a fight!

FN-2187 and Poe flew into space.
The First Order ship fired
on their TIE fighter!

Poe flew the TIE fighter.

FN-2187 fired back at the big ship.

FN-2187 and Poe escaped
from the First Order ship.

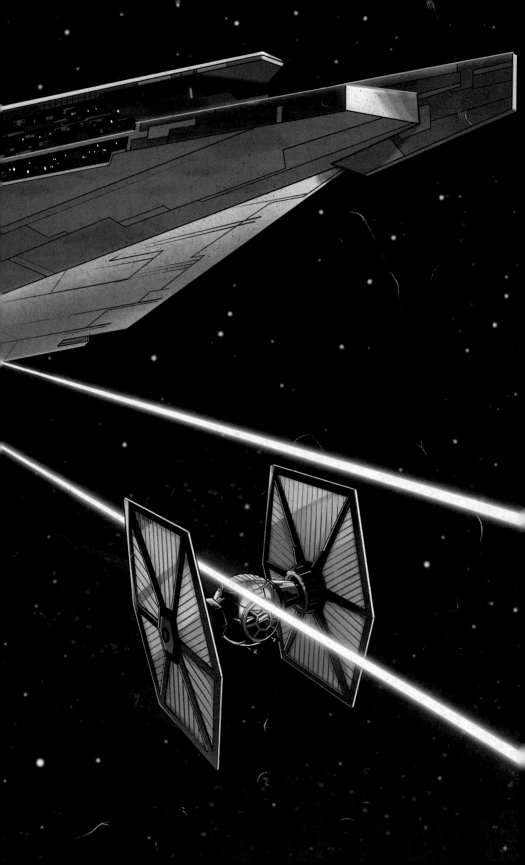

Poe was proud of his new friend.
Poe called him Finn.

Poe flew the TIE fighter toward Jakku.
He needed to find BB-8.

Finn and Poe made a great team!